The
Victim

Faber
Stories

P. D. James (1920–2014) was born in Oxford and educated at Cambridge High School for Girls. From 1949 to 1968 she worked in the National Health Service and subsequently in the Home Office, first in the Police Department and later in the Criminal Policy Department. All that experience was used in her novels. She was a Fellow of the Royal Society of Literature and of the Royal Society of Arts and served as a Governor of the BBC, a member of the Arts Council, where she was Chairman of the Literary Advisory Panel, on the Board of the British Council and as a magistrate in Middlesex and London. She was an Honorary Bencher of the Honourable Society of the Inner Temple. She won awards for crime writing in Britain, America, Italy and Scandinavia, including the Mystery Writers of America Grandmaster Award and The National Arts Club Medal of Honor for Literature (US). She received honorary degrees from seven British universities, was awarded an OBE in 1983 and was created a life peer in 1991. In 1997 she was elected President of the Society of Authors, stepping down from the post in August 2013.

P. D. James

The Victim

Faber Stories

ff

First published in this single edition in 2019
by Faber & Faber Limited
Bloomsbury House
74–77 Great Russell Street
London WC1B 3DA

First published in *Winter Crimes 5*, ed. Virginia Whitaker in 1973
First published by Faber in *Sleep No More* in 2017

Typeset by Faber & Faber Limited
Printed and bound by CPI Group (UK) Ltd, Croydon, CR0 4YY

The right of P. D. James to be identified as author of this work
has been asserted in accordance with Section 77 of the Copyright,
Designs and Patents Act 1988

A CIP record for this book
is available from the British Library

ISBN 978–0–571–35175–6

You know Princess Ilsa Mancelli, of course. I mean by that that you must have seen her on the cinema screen; on television; pictured in newspapers arriving at airports with her latest husband; relaxing on their yacht; bejewelled at first nights, gala nights, at any night and in any place where it is obligatory for the rich and successful to show themselves. Even if, like me, you have nothing but bored contempt for what I believe is called the international jet set, you can hardly live in the modern world and not know Ilsa Mancelli. And you can't fail to have picked up some scraps about her past. The brief and not particularly successful screen career, when even her heart-stopping beauty couldn't quite compensate for the paucity of talent; the succession of marriages – first to the producer who made her first film and who broke a twenty-year-old marriage to get her; then to a Texan millionaire; lastly to a prince. About two months ago I saw a nauseatingly sentimental picture of her with her two-day-old son in a Rome nursing home. So it looks as if this marriage, sanctified as it is by

1

wealth, a title and maternity, may be intended as her final adventure.

The husband before the film producer is, I notice, no longer mentioned. Perhaps her publicity agent fears that a violent death in the family, particularly an unsolved violent death, might tarnish her bright image. Blood and beauty. In the early stages of her career they hadn't been able to resist that cheap, vicarious thrill. But not now. Nowadays her early history, before she married the film producer, has become a little obscure, although there is a suggestion of poor but decent parentage and early struggles suitably rewarded. I am the most obscure part of that obscurity. Whatever you know, or think you know, of Ilsa Mancelli, you won't have heard about me. The publicity machine has decreed that I be nameless, faceless, unremembered, that I no longer exist. Ironically, the machine is right; in any real sense, I don't.

I married her when she was Elsie Bowman aged seventeen. I was assistant librarian at our local branch library and fifteen years older, a thirty-two-year-old virgin, a scholar manqué, thin-faced, a little stooping, my meagre hair already thinning. She worked on the cosmetic counter of our High Street store. She was beautiful then, but with a delicate, tentative, unsophisticated loveliness which gave little promise of the polished mature beauty which is hers today. Our story was very ordinary. She returned a book to the library one evening when I was on counter duty. We chatted. She asked my advice about novels for her mother. I spent as long as I dared finding suitable romances for her on the shelves. I tried to interest her in the books I liked. I asked her about herself, her life, her ambitions. She was the only woman I had been able to talk to. I was enchanted by her, totally and completely besotted.

I used to take my lunch early and make surreptitious visits to the store, watching her from the shadow of a neighbouring pillar. There is one picture which even now seems to stop my heart. She had dabbed her wrist with scent and was holding out a bare arm over the counter so that a prospective customer could smell the perfume. She was entirely absorbed, her young face gravely preoccupied. I watched her, silently, and felt the tears smarting my eyes.

It was a miracle when she agreed to marry me. Her mother (she had no father) was reconciled if not enthusiastic about the match. She didn't, as she made it abundantly plain, consider me much of a catch. But I had a good job with prospects; I was educated; I was steady and reliable; I spoke with a grammar-school accent which, while she affected to deride it, raised my status in her eyes. Besides, any marriage for Elsie was better than none. I was dimly aware when I bothered to think about Elsie in relation to anyone but myself that she and her mother didn't get on.

Mrs Bowman made, as she described it, a splash. There was a full choir and a peal of bells. The church hall was hired and a sit-down meal, ostentatiously unsuitable and badly cooked, was served to eighty guests. Between the pangs of nervousness and indigestion I was conscious of smirking waiters in short white jackets, a couple of giggling bridesmaids from the store, their freckled arms bulging from pink taffeta sleeves, hearty male relatives, red-faced and with buttonholes of carnation and waving fern, who made indelicate jokes and clapped me painfully between the shoulders. There were speeches and warm champagne. And, in the middle of it all, Elsie, my Elsie, like a white rose.

I suppose that it was stupid of me to imagine that I could hold her. The mere sight of our morning faces, smiling at each other's reflection in the bedroom mirror, should have warned me that it couldn't last. But, poor deluded fool, I never dreamed that I might lose her except by death. Her death I dared not contemplate, and I was afraid for the first time of my own. Happiness had made a coward of me. We moved into a new bungalow, chosen by Elsie, sat in new chairs chosen by Elsie, slept in a befrilled bed chosen by Elsie. I was so happy that it was like passing into a new phase of existence, breathing a different air, seeing the most ordinary things as if they were newly created. One isn't necessarily humble when greatly in love. Is it so unreasonable to recognise the value of a love like mine, to believe that the beloved is equally sustained and transformed by it?

She said that she wasn't ready to start a baby and, without her job, she was easily bored. She took a brief training in shorthand and typing at our local technical college and found herself a position as shorthand typist at the firm of Collingford and Major. That, at least, was how the job started. Shorthand typist, then secretary to Mr Rodney Collingford, then personal secretary, then confidential personal secretary; in my bemused state of uxorious bliss I only half-registered her progress from occasionally taking his dictation when his then secretary was absent to flaunting his gifts of jewellery and sharing his bed.

He was everything I wasn't. Rich (his father had made a fortune from plastics shortly after the war and had left the factory to his only son), coarsely handsome in a swarthy fashion, big-muscled, confident, attractive to women. He prided himself on taking what he wanted. Elsie must have been one of his easiest pickings.

Why, I still wonder, did he want to marry her? I thought at the time that he couldn't resist depriving a pathetic, underprivileged, unattractive husband of a prize which neither looks nor talent had qualified him to deserve. I've noticed that about the rich and successful. They can't bear to see the undeserving prosper. I thought that half the satisfaction for him was in taking her away from me. That was partly why I knew that I had to kill him. But now I'm not so sure. I may have done him an injustice. It may have been both simpler and more complicated than that. She was, you see – she still is – so very beautiful.

I understand her better now. She was capable of kindness, good humour, generosity even, provided she was getting what she wanted. At the time we married, and perhaps eighteen months afterwards, she wanted me. Neither her egoism nor her curiosity had been able to resist such a flattering, overwhelming love. But, for her, marriage wasn't permanency. It was the first and necessary step towards the kind of life she dreamt of and meant to have. She was kind to me, in bed and out, while I was what she wanted. But when she wanted someone else, then my need of her, my jealousy, my bitterness, she saw as a cruel and wilful denial of her basic right – the right to have what she wanted. After all, I'd had her for nearly three years. It was two years more than I had any right to expect. She thought so. Her darling Rodney thought so. When my acquaintances at the library learnt of the divorce I could see in their eyes that they thought so too. And she couldn't see what I was so bitter about. Rodney was perfectly happy to be the guilty party; they weren't, she pointed out caustically, expecting me to behave like a gentle-man. I wouldn't have to pay for the divorce. Rodney would see to that. I wasn't being asked to provide her with alimony. Rodney had more than enough. At one point she came close to bribing me with Rodney's money to let her go without fuss. And yet – was it really as simple as that? She had loved me, or at least needed me, for a time. Had she perhaps seen in me the father that she had lost at five years old?

During the divorce, through which I was, as it

were, gently processed by highly paid legal experts as if I were an embarrassing but expendable nuisance to be got rid of with decent speed, I was only able to keep sane by the knowledge that I was going to kill Collingford. I knew that I couldn't go on living in a world where he breathed the same air. My mind fed voraciously on the thought of his death, savoured it, began systematically and with dreadful pleasure to plan it.

A successful murder depends on knowing your victim, his character, his daily routine, his weaknesses, those unalterable and betraying habits which make up the core of personality. I knew quite a lot about Rodney Collingford. I knew facts which Elsie had let fall in her first weeks with the firm, typing-pool gossip. I knew the fuller and rather more intimate facts which she had disclosed in those early days of her enchantment with him, when neither prudence nor kindness had been able to conceal her obsessive preoccupation with her new boss. I should have been warned then. I knew, none better, the need to talk about the absent lover.

What did I know about him? I knew the facts that were common knowledge, of course. That he was wealthy, aged thirty, a notable amateur golfer; that he lived in an ostentatious mock Georgian house on the banks of the Thames looked after by overpaid but non-resident staff; that he owned a cabin cruiser; that he was just over six feet tall; that he was a good businessman but reputedly close-fisted; that he was methodical in his habits. I knew a miscellaneous and unrelated set of facts about him, some of which would be useful, some important, some of which I couldn't use. I knew – and this was rather surprising – that he was good with his hands and liked making things in metal and wood. He had built an expensively equipped and large workroom in the grounds of his house and spent every Thursday evening working there alone. He was a man addicted to routine. This creativity, however mundane and trivial, I found intriguing, but I didn't let myself dwell on it. I was interested in him only so far as his personality and habits were relevant to his death. I never thought of him as a human being. He had no existence for me apart from my hate. He was Rodney Collingford, my victim.

First, I decided on the weapon. A gun would have been the most certain, I supposed, but I didn't know how to get one and was only too well aware that I wouldn't know how to load or use it if I did. Besides, I was reading a number of books about murder at the time and I realised that guns, however cunningly obtained, were easy to trace. And there was another thing. A gun was too impersonal, too remote. I wanted to make physical contact at the moment of death. I wanted to get close enough to see that final look of incredulity and horror as he recognised, simultaneously, me and his death. I wanted to drive a knife into his throat.

I bought it two days after the divorce. I was in no hurry to kill Collingford. I knew that I must take my time, must be patient, if I were to act in safety. One day, perhaps when we were old, I might tell Elsie. But I didn't intend to be found out. This was to be the perfect murder. And that meant taking my time. He would be allowed to live for a full year.

But I knew that the earlier I bought the knife the more difficult it would be, twelve months later, to trace the purchase. I didn't buy it locally. I went one Saturday morning by train and bus to a north-east suburb and found a busy ironmongers and general store just off the High Street. There was a variety of knives on display. The blade of the one I selected was about six inches long and was made of strong steel screwed into a plain wooden handle. I think it was probably meant for cutting lino. In the shop its razor-sharp edge was protected by a thick cardboard sheath. It felt good and right in my hand. I stood in a small queue at the pay desk and the cashier didn't even glance up as he took my notes and pushed the change towards me.

But the most satisfying part of my planning was the second stage. I wanted Collingford to suffer. I wanted him to know that he was going to die. It wasn't enough that he should realise it in a last second before I drove in the knife or in that final second before he ceased to know anything for ever. Two seconds of agony, however horrible, weren't an adequate return for what he had done to me. I wanted him to know that he was a condemned man, to know it with increasing certainty, to wonder every morning whether this might be his last day. What if this knowledge did make him cautious, put him on his guard? In this country, he couldn't go armed. He couldn't carry on his business with a hired protector always at his side. He couldn't bribe the police to watch him every moment of the day. Besides, he wouldn't want to be thought a coward. I guessed that he would carry on, outwardly normal, as if the threats were unreal or derisory, something to laugh about with his drinking cronies. He was the sort to laugh at danger. But he would never be sure. And, by the end, his nerve and confidence would be broken. Elsie wouldn't know him for the man she had married.

I would have liked to have telephoned him, but that, I knew, was impracticable. Calls could be traced; he might refuse to talk to me; I wasn't confident that I could disguise my voice. So the sentence of death would have to be sent by post. Obviously, I couldn't write the notes or the envelopes myself. My studies in murder had shown me how difficult it was to disguise handwriting, and the method of cutting out and sticking together letters from a newspaper seemed messy, very time consuming and difficult to manage wearing gloves. I knew, too, that it would be fatal to use my own small portable typewriter or one of the machines at the library. The forensic experts could identify a machine.

And then I hit on my plan. I began to spend my Saturdays and occasional half-days journeying round London and visiting shops where they sold secondhand typewriters. I expect you know the kind of shop; a variety of machines of different ages, some practically obsolete, others hardly used, arranged on tables where the prospective purchaser may try them out. There were new machines too, and the proprietor was usually employed in demonstrating their merits or discussing hire-purchase terms. The customers wandered desultorily around, inspecting the machines, stopping occasionally to type out an exploratory passage. There were little pads of rough paper stacked ready for use. I didn't, of course, use the scrap paper provided. I came supplied with my own writing materials, a well-known brand sold in every stationers and on every railway bookstall. I bought a small supply of paper and envelopes once every two months and never from the same shop. Always, when handling them, I wore a thin pair of gloves, slipping them on as soon as my typing was complete. If someone were near, I would tap out the usual drivel about the sharp brown fox or all good men coming to the aid of the party. But if I were quite alone I would type something very different.

'This is the first comunication, Collingford. You'll be getting them regularly from now on. They're just to let you know that I'm going to kill you.'

'You can't escape me, Collingford. Don't bother to inform the police. They can't help you.'

'I'm getting nearer, Collingford. Have you made your will?'

'Not long now, Collingford. What does it feel like to be under sentence of death?'

The warnings weren't particularly elegant. As a librarian, I could think of a number of apt quotations which would have added a touch of individuality or style, perhaps even of sardonic humour, to the bald sentence of death. But I dared not risk originality. The notes had to be ordinary, the kind of threat which anyone of his enemies, a worker, a competitor, a cuckolded husband, might have sent.

Sometimes I had a lucky day. The shop would be large, well supplied, nearly empty. I would be able to move from typewriter to typewriter and leave with perhaps a dozen or so notes and addressed envelopes ready to send. I always carried a folded newspaper in which I could conceal my writing pad and envelopes and into which I could quickly slip my little stock of typed messages.

It was quite a job to keep myself supplied with notes and I discovered interesting parts of London and fascinating shops. I particularly enjoyed this part of my plan. I wanted Collingford to get two notes a week, one posted on Sunday and one on Thursday. I wanted him to come to dread Friday and

Monday mornings when the familiar typed envelope would drop on his mat. I wanted him to believe the threat was real. And why should he not believe it? How could the force of my hate and resolution not transmit itself through paper and typescript to his gradually comprehending brain?

I wanted to keep an eye on my victim. It shouldn't have been difficult; we lived in the same town. But our lives were worlds apart. He was a hard and sociable drinker. I never went inside a public house, and would have been particularly ill at ease in the kind of public house he frequented. But, from time to time, I would see him in the town. Usually he would be parking his Jaguar, and I would watch his quick, almost furtive look to left and right before he turned to lock the door. Was it my imagination that he seemed older, that some of the confidence had drained out of him?

Once, when walking by the river on a Sunday in early spring, I saw him manoeuvring his boat through Teddington Lock. Ilsa – she had, I knew, changed her name after her marriage – was with him. She was wearing a white trouser suit; her flowing hair was bound by a red scarf. There was a party. I could see two more men and a couple of girls and hear high female squeals of laughter. I turned quickly and slouched away as if I were the guilty one. But not before I had seen Collingford's face. This time I couldn't be mistaken. It wasn't, surely, the tedious job of getting his boat unscratched through the lock that made him appear so grey and strained.

The third phase of my planning meant moving house. I wasn't sorry to go. The bungalow, feminine, chintzy, smelling of fresh paint and the new shoddy furniture which she had chosen, was Elsie's home not mine. Her scent still lingered in cupboards and on pillows. In these inappropriate surroundings I had known greater happiness than I was ever to know again. But now I paced restlessly from room to empty room, fretting to be gone.

It took me four months to find the house I wanted. It had to be on or very near to the river within two or three miles upstream of Collingford's house. It had to be small and reasonably cheap. Money wasn't too much of a difficulty. It was a time of rising house prices and the modern bungalow sold at three hundred pounds more than I had paid for it. I could get another mortgage without difficulty if I didn't ask for too much, but I thought it likely that, for what I wanted, I should have to pay cash.

The house agents perfectly understood that a man on his own found a three-bedroom bungalow too large for him and, even if they thought me rather vague about my new requirements and irritatingly imprecise about the reasons for rejecting their offerings, they still sent me others to view. And then, suddenly on an afternoon in April, I found exactly what I was looking for. It actually stood on the river, separated from it only by a narrow towpath. It was a one-bedroom, shack-like wooden bungalow with a tiled roof, set in a small neglected plot of sodden grass and overgrown flower beds. There had once been a wooden landing stage but now the two remaining planks, festooned with weeds and tags of rotted rope, were half-submerged beneath the slime of the river. The paint on the small veranda had long ago flaked away. The wallpaper of twined roses in the sitting room was blotched and faded. The previous owner had left two old cane chairs and a ramshackle table. The kitchen was pokey and ill-equipped. Everywhere there hung a damp miasma of depression and decay. In summer, when the neighbouring shacks and bungalows were occupied by holidaymakers and weekenders, it would, no doubt, be cheerful enough. But in October, when I planned to kill Collingford, it would be as deserted and isolated as a disused morgue. I bought it and paid cash. I was even able to knock two hundred pounds off the asking price.

My life that summer was almost happy. I did my job at the library adequately. I lived alone in the shack, looking after myself as I had before my marriage. I spent my evenings watching television. The images flickered in front of my eyes almost unregarded, a monochrome background to my bloody and obsessive thoughts.

I practised with the knife until it was as familiar in my hand as an eating utensil. Collingford was taller than me by six inches. The thrust then would have to be upward. It made a difference to the way I held the knife and I experimented to find the most comfortable and effective grip. I hung a bolster on a hook in the bedroom door and lunged at a marked spot for hours at a time. Of course, I didn't actually insert the knife; nothing must dull the sharpness of its blade. Once a week, a special treat, I sharpened it to an even keener edge.

Two days after moving into the bungalow I bought a dark-blue untrimmed tracksuit and a pair of light running shoes. Throughout the summer I spent an occasional evening running on the towpath. The people who owned the neighbouring chalets – when they were there, which was infrequently – got used to the sound of my television through the closed curtains and the sight of my figure jogging past their windows. I kept apart from them and from everyone, and summer passed into autumn. The shutters were put up on all the chalets except mine. The towpath became mushy with fallen leaves. Dusk fell early, and the summer sights and sounds died on the river. And it was October.

He was due to die on Thursday October 17th, the anniversary of the final decree of divorce. It had to be a Thursday, the evening which he spent by custom alone in his workshop, but it was a particularly happy augury that the anniversary should fall on this day. I knew that he would be there. Every Thursday for nearly a year I had padded along the two and a half miles of the footpath in the evening dusk and had stood briefly watching the squares of light from his windows and the dark bulk of the house behind.

It was a warm evening. There had been a light drizzle for most of the day but, by dusk, the skies had cleared. There was a thin white sliver of moon and it cast a trembling ribbon of light across the river. I left the library at my usual time, said my usual goodnights. I knew that I had been my normal self during the day, solitary, occasionally a little sarcastic, conscientious, betraying no hint of the inner tumult.

I wasn't hungry when I got home but I made myself eat an omelette and drink two cups of coffee. I put on my swimming trunks and hung around my neck a plastic toilet bag containing the knife. Over the trunks I put on my track suit, slipping a pair of thin rubber gloves into the pocket. Then, at about quarter past seven, I left the shack and began my customary gentle trot along the tow path.

When I got to the chosen spot opposite to Collingford's house I could see at once that all was well. The house was in darkness but there were the expected lighted windows of his workshop. I saw that the cabin cruiser was moored against the boathouse. I stood very still and listened. There was no sound. Even the light breeze had died and the yellowing leaves on the riverside elms hung motionless. The towpath was completely deserted. I slipped into the shadow of the hedge where the trees grew thickest and found the place I had already selected. I put on the rubber gloves, slipped out of the tracksuit, and left it folded around my running shoes in the shadow of the

23

hedge. Then, still watching carefully to left and right, I made my way to the river.

I knew just where I must enter and leave the water. I had selected a place where the bank curved gently, where the water was shallow and the bottom was firm and comparatively free of mud. The water struck very cold, but I expected that. Every night during that autumn I had bathed in cold water to accustom my body to the shock. I swam across the river with my methodical but quiet breaststroke, hardly disturbing the dark surface of the water. I tried to keep out of the path of moonlight but, from time to time, I swam into its silver gleam and saw my red gloved hands parting in front of me as if they were already stained with blood.

I used Collingford's landing stage to clamber out the other side. Again I stood still and listened. There was no sound except for the constant moaning of the river and the solitary cry of a night bird. I made my way silently over the grass. Outside the door of his workroom, I paused again. I could hear the noise of some kind of machinery. I wondered whether the door would be locked, but it opened easily when I turned the handle. I moved into a blaze of light.

I knew exactly what I had to do. I was perfectly calm. It was over in about four seconds. I don't think he really had a chance. He was absorbed in what he had been doing, bending over a lathe, and the sight of an almost naked man, walking purposely towards him, left him literally impotent with surprise. But, after that first paralysing second, he knew me. Oh yes, he knew me! Then I drew my right hand from behind my back and struck. The knife went in as sweetly as if the flesh had been butter. He staggered and fell. I had expected that and I let myself go loose and fell on top of him. His eyes were glazed, his mouth opened and there was a gush of dark red blood. I twisted the knife viciously in the wound, relishing the sound of tearing sinews. Then I waited. I counted five deliberately, then raised myself from his prone figure and crouched behind him before withdrawing the knife. When I withdrew it there was a fountain of sweet-smelling blood which curved from his throat like an arch. There is one thing I shall never forget. The blood must have been red, what other colour could it have been? But, at the time and for ever afterwards, I saw it as a golden stream.

I checked my body for bloodstains before I left the workshop and rinsed my arms under the cold tap at his sink. My bare feet made no marks on the wooden-block flooring. I closed the door quietly after me and, once again, stood listening. Still no sound. The house was dark and empty.

The return journey was more exhausting than I had thought possible. The river seemed to have widened and I thought that I should never reach my home shore. I was glad I had chosen a shallow part of the stream and that the bank was firm. I doubt whether I could have drawn myself up through a welter of mud and slime. I was shivering violently as I zipped up my tracksuit, and it took me precious seconds to get on my running shoes. After I had run about a mile down the towpath I weighted the toilet bag containing the knife with stones from the path and hurled it into the middle of the river. I guessed that they would drag part of the Thames for the weapon but they could hardly search the whole stream. And, even if they did, the toilet bag was one sold at the local chain store which anyone might have bought, and I was confident that the knife could never be traced to me. Half an hour later I was back in my shack. I had left the television on and the news was just ending. I made myself a cup of hot cocoa and sat to watch it. I felt drained of thought and energy as if I had just made love. I was conscious of nothing but my tiredness, my body's coldness gradually returning to life in the warmth of the electric fire, and a great peace.

He must have had quite a lot of enemies. It was nearly a fortnight before the police got round to interviewing me. Two officers came, a Detective Inspector and a Sergeant, both in plain clothes. The Sergeant did most of the talking; the other just sat, looking round at the sitting room, glancing out at the river, looking at the two of us from time to time from cold grey eyes as if the whole investigation were a necessary bore. The Sergeant said the usual reassuring platitudes about just a few questions. I was nervous, but that didn't worry me.

They would expect me to be nervous. I told myself that, whatever I did, I mustn't try to be clever. I mustn't talk too much. I had decided to tell them that I spent the whole evening watching television, confident that no one would be able to refute this. I knew that no friends would have called on me. I doubted whether my colleagues at the library even knew where I lived. And I had no telephone so I need not fear that a caller's ring had gone unanswered during that crucial hour and a half.

On the whole it was easier than I had expected. Only once did I feel myself at risk. That was when the Inspector suddenly intervened. He said in a harsh voice:

'He married your wife didn't he? Took her away from you some people might say. Nice piece of goods, too, by the look of her. Didn't you feel any grievance? Or was it all nice and friendly? You take her, old chap. No ill feelings. That kind of thing.'

It was hard to accept the contempt in his voice but if he hoped to provoke me he didn't succeed. I had been expecting this question. I was prepared. I looked down at my hands and waited a few seconds before I spoke. I knew exactly what I would say.

'I could have killed Collingford myself when she first told me about him. But I had to come to terms with it. She went for the money you see. And if that's the kind of wife you have, well she's going to leave you sooner or later. Better sooner than when you have a family. You tell yourself "good riddance". I don't mean I felt that at first, of course. But I did feel it in the end. Sooner than I expected, really.'

That was all I said about Elsie then or ever. They came back three times. They asked if they could look round my shack. They looked round it. They took away two of my suits and the tracksuit for examination. Two weeks later they returned them without comment. I never knew what they suspected, or even if they did suspect. Each time they came I said less, not more. I never varied my story. I never allowed them to provoke me into discussing my marriage or speculating about the crime. I just sat there, telling them the same thing over and over again. I never felt in any real danger. I knew that they had dragged some lengths of the river but that they hadn't found the weapon. In the end they gave up. I always had the feeling that I was pretty low on their list of suspects and that, by the end, their visits were merely a matter of form.

It was three months before Elsie came to me. I was glad that it wasn't earlier. It might have looked suspicious if she had arrived at the shack when the police were with me. After Collingford's death I hadn't seen her. There were pictures of her in the national and local newspapers, fragile in sombre furs and black hat at the inquest, bravely controlled at the crematorium, sitting in her drawing room in afternoon dress and pearls with her husband's dog at her feet, the personification of loneliness and grief.

'I can't think who could have done it. He must have been a madman. Rodney hadn't an enemy in the world.'

That statement caused some ribald comment at the library. One of the assistants said, 'He's left her a fortune I hear. Lucky for her she had an alibi. She was at a London theatre all the evening, watching *Macbeth*. Otherwise, from what I've heard of our Rodney Collingford, people might have started to get ideas about his fetching little widow.'

Then he gave me a sudden embarrassed glance, remembering who the widow was.

And so one Friday evening, she came. She drove herself and was alone. The dark green Saab pulled up to my ramshackle gate. She came into the sitting room and looked around in a kind of puzzled contempt. After a moment, still not speaking, she sat in one of the fireside chairs and crossed her legs, moving one caressingly against the other. I hadn't seen her sitting like that before. She looked up at me. I was standing stiffly in front of her chair, my lips dry. When I spoke I couldn't recognise my own voice.

'So you've come back?' I said.

She stared at me, incredulous, and then she laughed:

'To you? Back for keeps? Don't be silly, darling! I've just come to pay a visit. Besides, I wouldn't dare

31

to come back, would I? I might be frightened that you'd stick a knife into my throat.'

I couldn't speak. I stared at her, feeling the blood drain from my face. Then I heard her high, rather childish voice. It sounded almost kind.

'Don't worry, I shan't tell. You were right about him, darling, you really were. He wasn't at all nice really. And mean! I didn't care so much about your meanness. After all, you don't earn so very much, do you? But he had half a million! Think of it, darling. I've been left half a million! And he was so mean that he expected me to go on working as his secretary even after we were married. I typed all his letters! I really did! All that he sent from home, anyway. And I had to open his post every morning unless the envelopes had a secret little sign on them he'd told his friends about to show that they were private.'

I said through bloodless lips:

'So all my notes—'

'He never saw them, darling. Well, I didn't want to worry him, did I? And I knew they were from you.

I knew when the first one arrived. You never could spell communication, could you? I noticed that when you used to write to the house agents and the solicitor before we were married. It made me laugh considering that you're an educated librarian and I was only a shop assistant.'

'So you knew all the time. You knew that it was going to happen.'

'Well, I thought that it might. But he really was horrible, darling. You can't imagine. And now I've got half a million! Isn't it lucky that I have an alibi? I thought you might come on that Thursday. And Rodney never did enjoy a serious play.'

After that brief visit I never saw or spoke to her again. I stayed in the shack, but life became pointless after Collingford's death. Planning his murder had been an interest, after all. Without Elsie and without my victim there seemed little point in living. And, about a year after his death, I began to dream. I still dream, always on a Monday and Friday. I live through it all again; the noise-less run along the towpath over the mush of damp leaves; the quiet swim across the river; the silent opening of his door; the upward thrust of the knife; the vicious turn in the wound; the animal sound of tearing tissues; the curving stream of golden blood. Only the homeward swim is different. In my dream the river is no longer a cleansing stream, luminous under the sickle moon, but a cloying, impenetrable, slow-moving bog of viscous blood through which I struggle in impotent panic towards a steadily re-ceding shore.

I know about the significance of the dream. I've read all about the psychology of guilt. Since I lost Elsie I've done all my living through books. But it doesn't help. And I no longer know who I am. I know who I used to be, our local assistant librarian, gentle, scholarly, timid, Elsie's husband. But then I killed Collingford. The man I was couldn't have done that. He wasn't that kind of person. So who am I? It isn't really surprising, I suppose, that the library committee suggested so tactfully that I ought to look for a less exacting job. A less exacting job than the post of assistant librarian? But you can't blame them. No one can be efficient and keep his mind on the job when he doesn't know who he is.

Sometimes, when I'm in a public house – and I seem to spend most of my time there nowadays since I've been out of work – I'll look over someone's shoulder at a newspaper photograph of Elsie and say:

'That's the beautiful Ilsa Mancelli. I was her first husband.'

I've got used to the way people sidle away from me, the ubiquitous pub bore, their eyes averted, their voices suddenly hearty. But sometimes, perhaps because they've been lucky with the horses and feel a spasm of pity for a poor deluded sod, they push a few coins over the counter to the barman before making their way to the door, and buy me a drink.